# Nursery!

## Lauren Tobia

They're so
tumbly,
wiggly,
jumbly!

Can YOU
do it, too?

Climb the steps, **DING DONG!**

The blue door opens wide.

Look! It's Bee and Billy,

About to go inside...

Children shout
and giggle,
Mummies hug goodbye.

Bee dashes off
   to play postmen,
Billy is hidey shy.

"Billy, look,"

says Postman Bee.

"This letter is

for you.

It says, 'Dear Billy,
Come to the farm,
There's lots of work
to do.'"

They drive the train together,

Clickety-clickety-CLACK!

The sheep say, "Baa!"

The cows say,

"Moo!"

What do the
ducks say?

"QUACK!"

Someone's got the tractor,

It's little Baby Boo!

Bee shouts,

"MINE!"

Then Baby cries,

Baby wants it,

too.

Clever big boy Billy,
Gives Baby Boo
his train.

Baby's giggly,
  smiley, dribbly,
Happy once again.

Now, what's that sniff-a-licious smell?

It's something really yummy...

**"Toast time!**

**Toast time!"**

Bee shouts out.

She has a rumbly tummy!

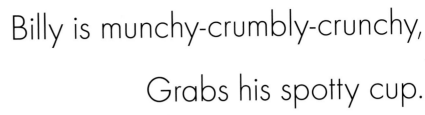

Billy is munchy-crumbly-crunchy,

Grabs his spotty cup.

Buttery fingers slip and slide,

Milky cup tips up!

Poor Billy! He starts to wail,

Grown-ups mop and fuss.

Bee says kindly, **"Share my drink.**

**There's enough for both of us."**

Then Bee and Billy build a tower,

Wibbly-wobbly tall.

Red and green and yellow blocks,

Can you count them all?

Little Baby Boo crawls past,
Blocks crash to the floor.
**"All fall down!"** claps Billy,
And they build it up
once more.

Billy finds a shaker.

**"Oh yes!"** shouts Bee.

**"Let's sing!"**

Bee and Billy jump
and dance,

Then everyone joins in!

Mummy's back! Let's tidy up,

There are coats and shoes to find.

And where have Billy's

socks gone?

We can't leave those behind!

Bee cries and shouts

and stamps her feet,

She wants to stay

and play.

But Mummy says,

"It's time to go,
You'll come back
another day."

Bee and Billy
are going home,
Today has been
such fun.

They're yawny,
sleepy, snuggly,
tired...

Goodbye,
everyone!